SUPERKIDS' CLUB

LIBRARY

The Odd Comics

Written by Valerie Tripp

Illustrated by Meryl Henderson

ROWLAND READING FOUNDATION

MIDDLETON, WISCONSIN

Memory Words

a   I   Oswald   the

Words to Sound Out

an	comic	glasses	grins
let's	not	rest	runs

To the adult: Memory Words are words the child has learned to recognize by sight alone. All other words in this story consist of sounds taught in class, and the child should be able to sound them out letter by letter. The Words to Sound Out listed above contain recently learned sounds and letters and may require additional reading practice.

Oswald and Ettabetta get set.

1

Ettabetta runs fast.
Oswald runs fast.

Ettabetta has fun.
Oswald has fun.

Ettabetta sits.
Oswald sits.

Let's rest.

Oswald gets a comic.
Ettabetta gets a comic.

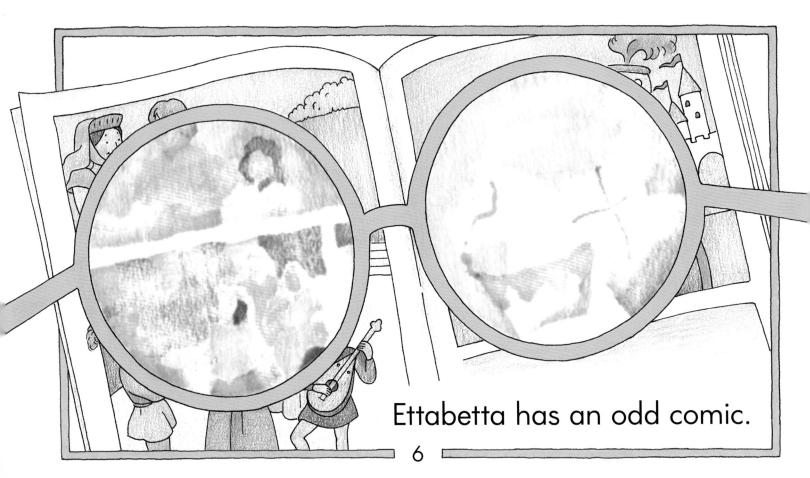

Ettabetta has an odd comic.

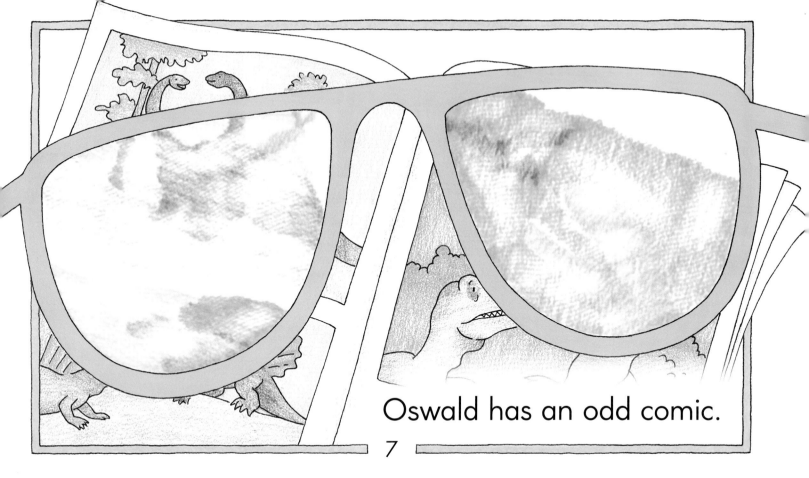

Oswald has an odd comic.